BROTHERS

TAKEN AWAY   NOT HOME FOR THE HOLIDAYS

THIS PLACE IS NOT MY HOME   JUST MAYBE

Please visit our website, www.west44books.com. For a free color catalog of all our high-quality books, call toll free 1-800-542-2595 or fax 1-877-542-2596.

Cataloging-in-Publication Data

Names: Bermudez, Cyn.
Title: Taken away / Cyn Bermudez.
Description: New York : West 44, 2019. | Series: Brothers
Identifiers: ISBN 9781538382295 (pbk.) | ISBN 9781538382301 (library bound) | ISBN 9781538383155 (ebook)
Subjects: LCSH: Foster home care--Juvenile fiction. | Electronic mail messages--Juvenile fiction. | Siblings--Juvenile fiction.
Classification: LCC PZ7.B476 Ta 2019 | DDC [E]--dc23

First Edition

Published in 2019 by
Enslow Publishing LLC
101 West 23rd Street, Suite #240
New York, NY 10011

Editor: Theresa Emminizer
Designer: Sam DeMartin

Printed in the United States of America

CPSIA compliance information: Batch #CS18W44: For further information contact
Enslow Publishing LLC, New York, New York at 1-800-542-2595.

BROTHERS

MISS YOU
COOKIES
SENSITIVE
TEARS
ISAAC
DREAMER
PUNCH
LONELY
SQUID

CHAPTER ONE
The Rice Mom Made

From: isaac-the-great@email.com
To: victory333@email.com
Subject: My new foster home!

My new foster mom made a rice dish. Like the one Momma makes. The sweet one. *Arroz con leche.* Only she called the dish something else. A Filipino word. The rice almost tasted like Momma's but without the cinnamon. Momma had arroz con leche on the stove that morning. When the police came. I had bugged her for it all week.

She was mad because I put too much cinnamon in it. I had only wanted to help. I'm sorry for that. For the way I'm annoying all the time. Maybe if I hadn't bugged her so much…

My new foster mom's name is Susan. John is my new foster dad. Susan always smells like Jergens lotion. John smells like Abuelo's cologne. Old Spice. I don't mind it. Their scents cover the cabbage and fish smell from downstairs. There is always cooked rice. The way Momma always made beans.

I cried when Susan served me her rice dish. I wiped the tears from my cheeks as fast as I could. But she knew. She asked me if I was okay. I didn't want to tell her anything. Just like we promised. They don't need to know our business! She told me not to be scared. I wasn't scared, Victor. I really wasn't. I just miss Momma so much. And you. And our sisters. Susan told me your foster home is 45 minutes away. Vanessa and Sara are 30 minutes away. I hate being so far from everyone. I might as well be on the other side of the world! Why can't we be together?

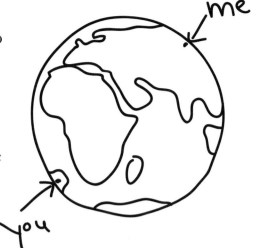

Seeing that rice dish made

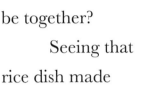

me miss Momma an awful lot. But it was more than that too. That day, when the cops came, I had just sat down to eat a hot bowl. I didn't care that Momma was mad about the cinnamon. That was my favorite part. You opened the door, remember? The officers scared me. The way they stomped into our apartment. Like their shoes were made of metal or something.

Susan thought maybe I was just sad because of Momma being gone. John told her not to pry. He pulled her into the next room to "discuss her tone." They were in the living room speaking with hushed words. I was in the kitchen. I could hear them, though. John told her to give me space. Susan thought I should be talking about what happened. She said not to bottle up my emotions. She said that's what makes people crazy.

I don't want to be crazy, Victor. I was tempted. I almost told Susan about the rice. About that morning when Momma was taken away. How the bowl fell to the floor when that officer came into our apartment. I almost told her how the bowl shattered. The rice splattered everywhere, even the ceiling! Momma would be so mad if she saw that mess. You would too. I would've cleaned up the mess, but those cops hauled us off. When we get home, I'll clean the rice good. I'll fix it. I promise. If we ever go home. Will we?

I didn't tell her anything. I was strong even though I was scared about the going crazy thing. I sucked up my tears. Swallowed them right down. I can be strong like you. I ignored her. Susan let it go after a few minutes of silence. She knew I wasn't going to crack. I was glad that John told her to give me space.

Everything is different here. Susan and John sound funny when they talk. You know how Momma speaks with an accent? Well, the Benavides are worse! They're always mixing "B" and "V" and Susan says "SHE" when she means "HE." John is always singing. There are all kinds of knickknacks around. Susan collects dolls. Even troll dolls. The porcelain dolls are the creepiest.

In the dark, sometimes I feel porcelain eyes staring at me. One time I heard shuffling feet behind me. When I turned around, no one was there. Susan and John have an old house. Upstairs, it smells like old carpet. The floorboards creak.

Last night was the worst. I couldn't sleep. I was anxious because I knew was I starting school today. School was different, too. There were a lot of white kids, some Filipinos like Susan and John, but only two other Mexican kids. I smiled at them, but they didn't even talk to me. I wanted to fade away. Disappear completely.

If I tell you something, you promise you won't get mad? Please don't be mad. Something happened at school today. Something bad.

I got into a fight. And not just words. I got into a fistfight. This white kid named Jake knew about Momma. Knew she was arrested and in prison, because of what she did. I don't know how he knew. He called Momma a name. I won't repeat it! It was rude and awful. The anger just boiled up to my brain. I couldn't think about anything. Not right or wrong or how I'd get punished.

I punched him. Right in the stomach, Victor. I gave him a good one, too. I heard the air push out of his mouth. I felt it push out of his stomach. He nearly dropped to the ground. He hunched over and cried. He cried a lot. My teacher was very angry. She kept shaking her head. She stared at me like I was some stray dog begging for scraps. I wanted to punch her, too. The anger left me. I sort of feel bad for that kid. All those tears he cried. But I also didn't care. He shouldn't have said what he did about Momma.

What's it like where you're at? I gotta go. I hear Susan calling me down to dinner.

TTYS

~ Isaac

P.S. John let me use an old Polaroid camera. The kind that spits instant pictures. It's so cool! John has a laptop and a scanner. So I can scan the Polaroid pictures. Check it out.

P.P.S. I wish we had cell phones. Email is for old people. And it's not enough.

1 Attachment

Filipino_Rice.jpg

CHAPTER TWO
A Witch's Face

From: victory333@email.com
To: isaac-the-great@email.com
Subject: Re: My new foster home!

A fight? I told you to stay out of trouble. Momma wouldn't like you fighting. She won't care about the rice. Not after everything that's happened.

But Momma will be okay. You'll see. They'll let her go. Then we will get to go home. All of us. Vanessa and Sara, too. You did good, Isaac. By not saying anything to your *foster keepers*.

They're your keepers! Not your parents. Not a mom or a dad. They're there to "keep" you in one piece until you're old enough to boot.

I have just one foster keeper. Her name is Cookie. But she wants me to call her Ms. Cutter. That's her name—COOKIE CUTTER. She said her momma named her that. Weird, huh? I wanted to say, *and…*? But didn't want to get mouthy. Momma always hated when I said that to her. Momma would tell me not to get mouthy. And I don't want any trouble. So I shut my mouth.

I waited for her to tell me more. Like her momma named her that because she was born in a donut store. Or while her mom was eating cookies. Or because…I don't know. I figured something weird like that. But she didn't. She just said, "My mother, God bless her soul, named me that."

And then she went on about Jax (that's her dog). Ms. Cutter is super old and her hair is gray.

She stinks like an ashtray and sounds like Fat Carl. Remember him? He used to fix cars with Dad before Dad died. Her voice is rough like his. Like sandpaper. Dad said it was because he smoked like a chimney.

Ms. Cutter talks a lot. Just not to me. Except to give me more chores. More and more, all the time. Do the dishes, sweep the floor, vacuum, dust. Does she do anything?

I guess I'm luckier than you, though. At least she doesn't try and get me to talk about Momma. If she did, I'd tell her to back off.

I'm sorry you got into a fight. I'm sorry that kid was mean to you about Momma. Are you scared? Maybe they'll finally place us together. That's what you say to your worker. That's the lady who took us from Momma. Maybe she'll finally see that we need to be together. I hope.

I like my new school. No one knows about Momma there. I'm glad for it. I made a few friends. We sit together far away from everyone, under an old tree. We call it "the field" because it's near the track field. You should see the tree we sit under. It's huge. The tree is really old. The bark on the trunk looks like an old witch's face.

Remember that story Momma told us? The one about an old witch who tried to eat a couple of kids in the forest? That's what I think of, anyway. I try not to look at the tree, but I can't help it. I have Dad's old camera. So I took a picture of it. Crazy, huh?

Anyway, I'm glad your keepers have a laptop you can use. Back home, we all had to share

Momma's old phone to go online, remember?

Ms. Cutter has a computer too. One of those desktop ones, like in old movies. It looks like a robot head.

I have to clean the living room if I want to eat dinner. There ain't ever enough around here. Vacuuming takes forever. Her vacuum doesn't work good.

TTYS
Victor

1 Attachment
Old_Witch_Tree.jpg

CHAPTER THREE
Eating Squid

From: isaac-the-great@email.com
To: victory333@email.com
Subject: I ate squid

Yikes! That tree is scary! The witch face looks really mean. I wouldn't want to sit near that tree. Maybe I would if I had friends. I don't have any friends at my new school.

I remember the story Momma read. "Hansel and Gretel." The story was about a brother and sister getting lost in the woods. That's when the witch finds them. Momma would act out the story. When she read the part of the witch, she'd make her voice sound old. Then she'd laugh like a witch. She always had the best stories.

I don't have a lot of chores. Just keep my room clean. I help John with the yard sometimes. Sometimes I offer to help clean other rooms. Susan always says it's okay. There's a lot of food here. I wish I could give you some.

Most of the food is good. Susan cooks all the time. She's always cooking fish or seafood. Like shrimp. One time she made little octopuses! John said they were squids, not octopuses. The squids had a lot of legs. The legs looked weird.

Tentacles—that's what John called the legs. The tentacles had a bunch of tiny suction cups on them. Susan told me to try it. I didn't want to. She said, "How do you know you don't like it, if you don't try it?" Made sense. I tasted the squid. It was chewy. I gagged a little bit. She didn't make me eat any more of it. She made me a peanut butter and jelly sandwich instead.

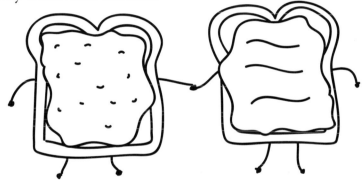

I spoke with the worker. She said they'd move me to a different place if I kept having trouble. She said I won't be with you, though. I don't wanna move. I like it here. I mean, I'd rather be with Momma and you and Vanessa and Sara. Or even with just you, if they'd let me. But if I'm going to be away from you all, I'd rather be here. Susan and John sound funny and smell funny. But they're nice to me. I don't mind the weird food.

I don't mind that Susan tries to talk to me about Momma. Maybe I can talk to her about some things. Like how much I miss Momma. I do miss Momma an awful lot. Susan hugs me when I cry. I know I'm too old for that. I know 11-year-olds shouldn't cry like babies. But still, Susan's hug makes me feel better.

I hate my new school. The kids there are mean. They're jerks. More kids are saying mean things about Momma. They say mean things about me, too. They say I'll end up in jail! I don't want to go to jail.

I eat my lunch in the bathroom. I hide in a stall. I pick my legs up and breathe real quiet. I'm afraid I'll get angry again and punch someone. If I do that, they'll send me away.

Will they send me to jail? Same one as

Momma?

I miss my friends at my old school. I miss my teacher. I miss our room and our video games. I miss you. I even miss Vanessa and Sara, even though I used to think our little sisters were annoying. I miss Momma most of all.

I better go to bed now.

TTYS
~ Isaac

P.S. I'm going to have a foster brother. Wish it could be you.

2 Attachments
Little_Squid.jpg
PB&J.jpg

CHAPTER FOUR
A Dead Thing

From: victory333@email.com
To: isaac-the-great@email.com
Subject: I'm hunting a werewolf!!!!

You're not going to jail, dummy. You have to do something *really* bad. Like a crime. Fighting is *not* good. But not a crime.

And what do you mean, foster "brother"? They are NOT your family. I worry about you. You're getting too comfortable with Susan and John. Your keepers are getting a new paycheck.

That's it. Ms. Cutter calls me her paycheck. That's what we are to them. They keep us. Make sure we are safe and alive until we're old enough. Then the State don't have to worry about us. I don't wanna be mean. I want you to keep to yourself. Don't tell Susan anything about how you feel. Because if you do, you'll get sadder. Momma needs us to be brave.

Ms. Cutter's got three of us. Me, a black kid named George, and a white girl named Michelle. Michelle is the oldest. She's almost 18. She doesn't talk to me except to call me a worm. Sometimes she yells at me to get out of her way. She says, "Move, worm." She's always

on the phone. It doesn't matter what she's doing. Chores, eating, watching TV. I think she even showers with the phone.

She talks on her cell phone even more than

Ms. Cutter talks. Except when Ms. Cutter is talking about the neighbor down the street. Ms. Cutter will talk to anyone who'll listen about old Mr. Burns. Momma would call her a gossip.

Mr. Burns is creepy, though. He's got a bunch of dried trees in front of his place. The paint on his house is peeling. Looks like he never waters the yard. He only comes out to get his mail. Walks real slow, too. Ms. Cutter thinks he's some kind of zombie. Like I said, creepy. I pass his house on the way to school. I make sure to run fast!

George is 16. George told me if I don't fuss, Ms. Cutter won't pay any attention to me. He said that was a good thing. Then I could do whatever I want. He said just don't get caught and do my chores. He told me the same thing you did. The worker will move you if you get in trouble a lot. George said it happened to him three times! Twice for getting in trouble. Another time they moved him when he hadn't done anything wrong.

Anyway, that's squid, huh? That thing looks really weird. Squid might be better than what I eat here. Ms. Cutter makes the same old food. We get cereal for breakfast—the generic O's with no sugar. A bologna sandwich for lunch. Dinner is some kind of meat with instant mashed potatoes. It's usually meatloaf or hot dogs. Have you ever heard of dried milk? She serves me watery milk made from a powder! Now that's gross. Yuck!

I do what George told me. I stay out of trouble and do my chores. Ms. Cutter pays no attention to me, mostly. I might as well be invisible. I spend my spare time with one of my new friends. His name is Lucky. You'd like Lucky. His real name is Lucas. But everyone calls him Lucky. He's funny, and has a really loud laugh. He lives down the street. Lucky thinks Mr. Burns is "supernatural." I asked him, "Like a zombie?" Because Ms. Cutter said he was dead. Lucky said no. According to this blog he read, Mr. Burns might be a shape-shifter.

Like a werewolf. There are a lot of rabbits in this area. That would be plenty of food for Mr. Burns.

Here, check it out: http://www.compendium-of-the-undead.com/how-to-tell-if-your-neighbor-is-a-werewolf.html

Lucky thinks we should go exploring. See if we can find evidence. That way we can help the neighborhood and the rabbits! He wants to investigate tomorrow morning. We'll probably take Jax with us.

Jax is a nice-looking dog, huh? He loves jumping and playing. He follows me around everywhere. Lucky thinks Jax will be a big help. He said all the best detectives have dogs. Jax'll help us find rabbit bones. There should be a lot of 'em if that's what Mr. Burns eats.

All this talk of eating has made me hungry. I wish I could eat that peanut butter and jelly! Lots of peanut butter, just how I like it. My stomach will have to settle for a bologna sandwich. You know what sounds good? Momma's rice and pork. Meatball soup and homemade tortillas. Fried chicken and real mashed potatoes. Fried beans, bacon, eggs, cereal with sugar, real milk!

Ugh! Now my stomach is growling. I gotta get going. I need to eat.

One last thing I want you to know. Stop being afraid. I don't want you fighting, but I don't want you hiding either. It's okay to stand up for yourself. The worker won't move you for that. At least I don't think. Only if you do something real bad. Or if you keep on fighting. I don't know for sure what the worker will do.

What I do know is this. The teasing gets worse if you don't stand up. Try not to fight. But don't let anyone bully you either. If you have to, if you're pushed, then fight. If you fight, punch whoever real good. Might as well, if you're going to get in trouble anyway.

And stop crying so much! I miss Momma, too. I miss you and our sisters and our apartment. I miss our car. I miss my room and all my old stuff. I miss the smell of our apartment and Momma's perfume. I miss my old school. I miss my old friends. I even miss my old teachers!

Be strong, Isaac. Be strong for Momma.

TTYS
Victor

3 Attachments
Jax.jpg
Powdered_Milk.jpg
Creepy_Werewolf_Dead-Guy's_House.jpg

CHAPTER FIVE
God Just Is

From: isaac-the-great@email.com
To: victory333@email.com
Subject: I made a friend!

Victor, I said foster "brother" because what do I call him? Susan and John called him my brother. When I said, "He's not my brother," John said they didn't mean it like that.

Anyway, his name is Eric. I just call him that—Eric. He is back and forth. Sometimes he is back with his mom. Sometimes he is with Susan and John. He's 11, too. We go to the same school. He made friends already. Can you believe it? He even made friends with the guy I punched!

Eric's hair is orange, like a carrot. He's got a lot of freckles, too. I'm not sure what I think of him just yet. He seems nice, but he doesn't talk to me at school.

I stopped hiding at lunch, like you said. I eat by myself most of the time. Stephanie sits with me when she's there. We're in the same homeroom. She's real smart, knows a lot of stuff. You'd like her. She's a girl, but she's cool. We talk about basketball. She knows about Momma.

I didn't say anything though! The whole school seems to know. Stephanie showed me a news article online. It was all about Momma. How she was a housekeeper who stole lots of money and things from rich people who hired her. She looked tired and sad in her mug shot.

But the article didn't say how Momma

needed the money for our rent. It didn't say she did it for our family. She's not a bad person. Right, Victor?

I don't know how Jake knew that she was my mom. He told everybody else. He's the one I punched. Stephanie doesn't like him. Jake's always teasing her about her curly hair.

I showed Stephanie the picture of that dead guy. The one you sent of Mr. Burns. Yeah, his face is creepy. His skin folds and folds. He's got beady eyes and wrinkles on his neck. Stay away!

Stephanie says there's no such thing as "supernatural." She says I have an "overactive imagination." Momma used to love supernatural stories. We all did. She told the best stories. She'd believe you about Mr. Burns.

But Stephanie says Mr. Burns is just grumpy and old. She says we're supposed to respect old people. She says God is watching. I told her, "How come you believe in God. Ain't *He* supernatural?"

Stephanie said no. She said, "God just *is*."
Victor…do we believe in God?
Stephanie kept asking me that. I
told her I don't know. She asked,
"How come you don't know?" I told
her Momma would take us to church
twice a year. We went every Christmas
and Easter Sunday. We never studied
the Bible. Not like her family. They have
Bible study. They study it, like school study. She
invited me to go. I told her no since I wasn't sure
if we believe in God. Stephanie said it was good to
believe in something. That believing in something
will help Momma.

I asked her, "So if I believe in…Spiderman,
will that help my mom?" She got mad. She said
God doesn't work like that.

Susan and John believe in God. They have
crosses hanging in every room. I asked Susan
about God. She invited me to go with her to

church. I said no to Susan, too. John said God was a personal choice. He said going to church didn't mean Momma would be free. He said church helped people cope. I told him I didn't know what that meant. He said it was doing something that helped us feel less sad. I told him I'd rather play basketball. He said that was okay, too.

Besides, maybe you're right and Stephanie is wrong. Maybe Mr. Burns is a werewolf. He'd eat more than rabbits! Don't bother him either way.

I know you miss Momma, too. Sometimes I miss her so much, my chest hurts. Remember when we went bowling with Dad on his birthday? It was right before he died. Remember how hard it was to throw that ball? Because it was so heavy. When I think of Momma, I feel that heaviness. It's like that bowling ball is sitting on my chest. No matter how hard I try, I can't move it. I can't swallow it. I can't spit it out. That's when the tears come out.

I try to stop them. I really do.

I gulp at the air. I push my tears down as far as they can go. Sometimes it's too hard, and I can't stop them. They just well up in my eyes. I wipe the tears as fast as I can. My eyes turn red. Susan always notices the redness of my eyes.

I know Susan is not my mom. And John is not Dad. They are my keepers, like you said. It's just…when the tears come…

Don't be mad at me. I let Susan see me cry.

The kid I punched, Jake, has a lot of friends. They won't leave me alone. They say awful things about Momma and me. I don't hide in the bathroom anymore, like I said. For you, and because they follow me. It doesn't matter where I go. The last time, Susan was there. She picked me up from school. One of Jake's friends was saying stuff. Susan overheard. She didn't say anything when I got in the car. She didn't say anything on the ride home either. I thought maybe she hadn't heard anything. When we went inside the house, she asked me, "Is everything okay?"

I wanted to say yes. I stood silent. It seemed like forever. My chest felt heavy again. Like a bowling ball. I swallowed my spit. I gasped for air, but it kept me from crying. Then she hugged me. It reminded me of the way Momma would hug. She was warm and soft. The tears gushed out of my eyes. My eyes were water hoses. Susan is not a mom, but she felt like one.

Once I started crying, I couldn't stop. I cried

31

and cried. For two whole hours. Susan held me until I stopped. My eyes stung. My face was hot. Don't be mad.

1 Attachment
Stephanie_(look-at-her-crazy-hair!).jpg

CHAPTER SIX
The Faster Tomorrow Will Come

From: victory333@email.com
To: isaac-the-great@email.com
Subject: It's time to investigate!

Isaac, stop crying. Think of the good. Momma would say that. Whenever things went bad, she'd remind us of the good.

Remember when Momma finally took us to that carnival? The one we'd been on about? We begged and begged. She was always working. Never had any time. Then out of nowhere she called in sick. We drove 45 minutes. To the edge of town. We were so excited. Talking about which rides we were going to go on first. No one thought to check to see if it was open!

Remember how we cried 'cause it was closed? What did Momma say? She said, "Think of the good." She talked and talked. For 30 minutes! We found that run-down pizza place. Man, that place was ugly. It only had three tables and mismatched chairs. The woman that worked there looked like Aunt Dolores. She had big chubby cheeks. Momma gave us quarters to play the pinball machine. You beat me! The pizza was the best we'd ever had.

We ended up having a lot of fun that day. When you're at school, say it to yourself. Think of the good. You made a friend. That is good. She's got crazy hair! I like her already.

I try and focus on the good too. I hang out with Lucky every chance I get. Lucky and I are going to Mr. Burns' tomorrow! We have our bag of werewolf junk ready. Here is our checklist:

  • really old mirror (It belonged to Lucky's great-grandma!)

  • a silver necklace (We think it's silver. Lucky says the color will do.)

  • some tobacco (We took Cutter's cigarettes, ha!)

  • weird dog whistle (I can't tell if it works????)

  • long rope (I hope it's long enough!)

I know what you're thinking. Mirrors are for vampires. Lucky said we could still use it. Because if Mr. Burns *is* dead, he might not have a reflection. I figure it doesn't hurt to try. Our official plan is this:

- We'll draw him out with the whistle.
- Then make him weak with the silver. (I don't know how this works. Maybe throw the necklace at him?)
- Last, we'll tie him up.

I don't what the tobacco is for. Lucky just said to put it on the list. Maybe it will cover our human scent? Lucky made a map of Mr. Burns' house and yard. He's got a big, creepy house. Anyway, Lucky and I go at dawn. Wish us luck. :)

I better get to bed. Remember what Dad would say when we were excited about something? The faster you go to sleep, the faster tomorrow will come.

Love,
Victor

P.S. Don't cry anymore. You hear me? Momma wouldn't like it. And we promised each other—no keepers in our heads! Now she's in your head. You'll start acting like she's your momma. You won't remember our real momma anymore. We need to keep Momma in our heads.

6 Attachments
Mirror.jpg
Necklace.jpg
Tobacco.jpg
Weird-dog-whistle.jpg
Rope.jpg
Map.jpg

CHAPTER SEVEN
Tonight, We Sleep

From: isaac-the-great@email.com
To: victory333@email.com
Subject: My final hours

That pizza was so good! I forgot the name of that place. I remember the pizza, though. Extra sauce. Double pepperoni. Great, now my stomach is growling. 😫 👉 🍕

Bothering Mr. Burns is a bad idea. Aren't you worried you'll get in trouble?

Don't answer that. Knowing you, probably not.

I wish I could be more like you. You're not afraid of anything. Maybe I'll be that way when I'm 12, too.

I mean, I'm not scared like a little kid. But I'm kind of scared (just a tiny amount) all the time! Having Stephanie helps. But she's just a girl. She can't stop Jake. Or his friends. You're lucky to have Lucky. Maybe if I had someone like Lucky. Or better, if you were here…things would be better for me.

There is nothing I can do! Jake and his friends won't stop. Now Eric says stuff too. He says things when Susan and John aren't around. They go on and on about Momma. About me, and you too. Eric said I'll never see you or Momma ever again. He said Vanessa and Sara won't even remember me. You told me not to hide. You told me to stand up for myself. Well, I punched Jake, and he didn't stop. He's worse.

Lunchtime is the hardest. Stephanie and I were hanging out behind the gym during lunch. We were out in the open. Stephanie said technically we weren't hiding. We just stay out of sight. It worked for a while. I finally had some peace at school. But now Jake and his friends found that place, too!

I want to stay out of trouble. It's hard. They won't leave me alone. Now everyone is saying stuff. There are rumors about Jake and his friends. They are going to jump me. Stephanie said it's because the first punch was a sucker punch. So it didn't count. That's why Jake won't leave me alone. His friends back him up. Stephanie said fight him face-to-face. Then they will leave me alone. But

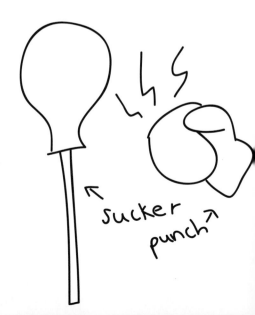

sucker punch

I already punched him face-to-face! She said no. Jake wasn't expecting it. So, it was a sucker punch.

If I'm going to stick up for myself, it's now or never. I'm going to fight Jake. *Before* he has a chance to jump me. I asked Stephanie if jumping was like sucker punching. She said no. I don't see why not. Since they'll do it when I'm not expecting it. Stephanie said but I am expecting it. She said, "We're talking about it. Right now! Duh."

The fight is on. Tomorrow at the mall. While you're investigating Mr. Burns, I'll be fighting for my life. Okay, maybe I am scared just like a little kid. Just as scared as the day they took Momma.

:(

mr.
Burns!
﬩

I wish you were here.

Love you, Victor.

~Isaac

P.S. I don't want to sleep. I don't want tomorrow to come.

P.P.S. What time are you investigating? There's a full moon.

P.P.P.S. I'm still hungry for pizza!!!

CHAPTER EIGHT
When the Moon Is Full

From: victory333@email.com
To: isaac-the-great@email.com
Subject: TROUBLE

Ugh! Mr. Burns is NOT a werewolf. Me and Lucky made him real mad. Now I'm in big trouble.

This is what happened. Lucky and I watched and waited in a field. The field across the street from his house. We hid in the bushes. Lucky blew on the whistle. I fanned the smoke from the tobacco. I had put the tobacco in aluminum foil. I used Ms. Cutter's matches to burn the tobacco.

Since it was Saturday, we got there late morning. We waited all day, until dark. Lucky and I thought he was hiding or something.

Lucky said, "Maybe he's *preparing*." Like Mr. Burns was planning his meal for the full moon. Then I started to worry. What if he ate us?

We started getting hungry and thirsty. We ate the cereal bars Lucky packed. I brought two water bottles. We drank them both. Then the sun started to set. My stomach growled. I was still hungry. I was glad Lucky had some cash. We walked to the Circle K quick. We both ate hot dogs. We drank Coke. Then we went back.

We hid in the bushes again. It got dark. We were about to give up. Finally, Mr. Burns came outside. He opened the door slowly. I saw his hand first and then his face. I thought he turned into a werewolf already. I swear I saw a furry hand. Lucky said, "He'll turn when he sees the moon."

Either way, we both panicked. Lucky and I came running out of the bushes. We both screamed. I threw the silver necklace at him. Lucky threw the rope at him.

Mr. Burns almost fell! We surprised him. He stumbled over his feet. He yelled! He grabbed me and Lucky by our shoulders. He brought us into his house. His house smelled like cookies. He was baking. Mr. Burns bakes???!!!

He called Ms. Cutter. Now she is real mad too. She lectured me for three hours.

She's talking about "returning" me. And she gave me more chores. Didn't think it was possible. I already do almost everything! She kept saying that we could have hurt Mr. Burns.

I said, "But we didn't." That only made her
madder. Now I'm grounded.

I also hope you DON'T have to fight Jake.
If you do, don't let him catch you off guard. Be
smart. Be brave.

TTYS
Victor

From: victory333@email.com
To: isaac-the-great@email.com
Subject: Re: TROUBLE

Hello? Everything okay?

From: victory333@email.com
To: isaac-the-great@email.com
Subject: Re: Re: TROUBLE

Where are you? Did something happen??

From: victory333@email.com
To: isaac-the-great@email.com
Subject: Re: Re: Re: TROUBLE

ISAAC?!

From: victory333@email.com
To: isaac-the-great@email.com
Subject: Re: Re: Re: Re: TROUBLE

I'm scared. Why haven't you written back? I love you, Isaac. I hope you're okay.

CHAPTER NINE
No More Shortcuts

From: isaac-the-great@email.com
To: victory333@email.com
Subject: Re: Re: Re: Re: TROUBLE

Don't worry! I'm alive! I was grounded, too.
Jake and I fought. It's not what you think, though.

I was on my way to meet him at the mall.
The mall is only three blocks from where I live. I
decided to walk there. I shouldn't have done that. I
stopped at Stephanie's apartment first. She said she
wanted to go with me. Stephanie said we should

take a shortcut. We'd get there faster. I wanted to get to the mall first. So I said yes.

Jake and his friends followed me! I didn't see them until we got to the alley. They started calling me names. Then Jake pushed me. Then they all started pushing me. Jake had three friends with him. Stephanie tried to help me. There were too many of them. Stephanie ran to get help.

It felt like forever. They hit me hard. I thought a tooth fell out. My nose crunched. I felt wetness on my face. I didn't cry. I fought back even though I was on the ground. I heard Stephanie calling my name. She sounded far away. She came with Susan and John. Jake and his friends ran when they saw Susan and John.

Susan was so worried. She hugged me tight. But she was mad too. They didn't yell at me. They were the opposite of Ms. Cutter. They were silent.

John took the laptop from the den. He put it away in their room. I couldn't email you!

They didn't talk to me for a long time. They only told me when it was time to eat, sleep, or go to school. Silence for a whole week. I really missed Momma then. Only she would know how to make me feel better. She'd never give me the silent treatment.

Jake and his friends weren't at school. Stephanie must have told Susan and John who they were. I think Stephanie told the principal. I overheard others talking. Jake and his friends were suspended. They got in big trouble.

I got in trouble, too. At first, I was mad at Susan and John. Why was I in trouble?! Wasn't *I* the one who was jumped? When Susan and John spoke finally spoke to me, they told me why. They didn't yell though.

Stephanie had told them where we were going. And why we were going there. John said, "Any kind of violence is wrong." He said I was wrong, too. Because I was going to fight.

Susan said I didn't make the right choices. Susan said they were disappointed in me. That made me sad. Sadder than any punishment. I don't know why. I told them what you said. That I had to stick up for myself. If I didn't, they'd always pick on me. And look what happened! They sucker punched me!

John said I should always try and talk things out. He said that was the mature thing to do. Now I put them in a "difficult position." John said they were grounding me because I was intending to fight. They spoke with Jake's parents. And the parents of the other kids. John said those kids will leave me alone now. I hope so.

They called my caseworker! Can you believe it? We are going to her office for a visit. They might move me to a new home. I don't want to leave here unless it's with you! What if I end up in a place worse than this one? Stephanie said some foster homes have a dozen kids! She said they have it rough! What if that happens to me?! I wish I never agreed to meet Jake at the mall. I wish I never went into that alley.

I've been cleaning. Staying quiet. I was grounded for two weeks. After, John put the laptop back in the den. I waited a few days before I got back on. I'm sorry I scared you.

:(

~ Isaac

P.S. Look at this crazy black eye.

1 Attachment
Black-eye.jpg

CHAPTER TEN
What We Need

From: victory333@email.com
To: isaac-the-great@email.com
Subject: We might see each other!

    Caseworker called. Ms. Cutter said, "You and your brother are two troublemaking peas in a pod."

Ms. Cutter told the caseworker about what Lucky and I did. We have a meeting too. I think we are all meeting at the caseworker's office.

This might be a good thing. Now you have a chance to beg our caseworker again. Ask her to keep us together. If I was there with you, that Jake kid wouldn't have dared.

What day and time are you going to be there?

I feel bad for what Lucky and I did. I mean, I guess a part of me knew Mr. Burns wasn't really a werewolf. Or a zombie. Or anything. But I felt like I believed it.

Maybe I just needed something to get my mind off Momma. Maybe I needed something to believe in. Maybe I was looking for trouble.

Still, I shouldn't have bothered Mr. Burns. I saw him the other day. He was limping. I think we might have hurt him by accident. It happened so fast. We didn't mean to hurt anyone.

Let's make a plan. We have to get our caseworker to keep us together.

Remember she said that keeping siblings together was what they tried for? I'll remind her she said that. We both should remind her. I think we have a good chance. I hope.

I can't take this anymore! This is hard. It's too much. When Dad died, that was hard. Our lives changed that day. I thought we'd never be happy again. I thought we'd never be normal again.

After a year we started to feel…a little normal. After two years, we were happy again. Not happy like when Dad was alive. But happy enough.

Why did this happen to *our* family? Why did Momma have to be taken away? Then *they*—Ms. Cutter calls *them* the "State"—separated us. Our family was pulled apart. It wasn't right then. It's not right now.

A family should be together. Or at least what

is left of a family. Momma may be gone for a long time. I know it scares you to hear that, but it's true. Me, you, Vanessa, and Sara should be together. Or least brother with brother, sister with sister.

I was really scared when you didn't write back. I thought something happened to you! I thought I'd never see you again. It made my stomach hurt bad. I even prayed. I don't ever want to feel that way again.

So we have to make this work. We have to get the caseworker to hear us. I have to go now.

Don't forget!

Don't ever forget.

TTYS

Victor

P.S. I kept this pic with me. Do you remember this? That was your favorite park when you were little. Dad made sure we had your sixth birthday there. Only our family was there. Best birthday party ever!

1 Attachment

park_photo.jpg

CHAPTER ELEVEN
Peanut Butter Cookies

From: isaac-the-great@email.com
To: victory333@email.com
Subject: Will I see you Monday?

    I didn't mean to scare you. I wanted to email you so bad. But I didn't want to sneak. Yes, I remember that birthday party. I miss those days. I wish things weren't so messed up. 😟

    My appointment for the caseworker is Monday. I'll be there in the morning. Susan said 9 a.m. Susan also said we might not see each other.

We are there the same day but not the same time. That doesn't make any sense! It's like they don't even want us to see each other.

Sometimes, I want to run away! I like Susan and John. But they could never be my family. I just want to hide. I wanna hide with you and Momma and our sisters.

Stephanie said she knew someone who did. She knew an older girl who ran away from her foster mom. Can you believe it? The older girl used to be her babysitter. I asked her what happened to her. Stephanie said she doesn't know. She said that one day, she left. No one heard from her again. Stephanie thinks probably nothing good.

I can't stop thinking about Monday. John said not to worry. Susan said not to worry, too. Susan and John are not sending me away. They told me. They don't want to send me away. She said they just want to make sure I'm okay. They have to because I was beat up. Maybe that's why you have to see the caseworker. Because Mr. Burns was hurt.

Mr. Burns will be okay. I hope you don't get into too much trouble. I got an idea! You know how he likes to bake? Why don't you bake him something? Like cookies or something like that. Then say you're sorry. Momma always stopped being mad when we said sorry. It didn't matter how mad she got.

I'd make cookies for Mr. Burns if I could.

I wouldn't have said it when Momma was around. I'll say it now, though…I liked to bake with Momma. 😌 I know it's girly. But I don't care anymore.

I liked baking cookies and cakes and pies. Peanut butter cookies were my favorite. Hey… make peanut butter cookies! I can't help you bake. BUT I remember the recipe. Here it is:

Ingredients

1 cup peanut butter

1 cup white sugar

1 egg

Instructions

Mix all together until gooey.

Don't forget to grease the pan!

Put spoonfuls of cookie mix onto the pan.

Flatten with a fork (like an X).

Bake at 350 degrees.

Bake for six to eight minutes.

Are you going to try? Ask Lucky to help you. Tell Lucky to say sorry, too!

TTYS—hopefully on Monday!

~ Isaac

P.S. I don't know if I explained it right.

P.P.S. I Googled the recipe! www.easy-cookies.com/pb-cookies.html

P.P.P.S. I really, really, really hope I see you Monday!!!!

1 Attachment

Peanut-butter-cookies.jpg

CHAPTER TWELVE
Moving Again

From: victory333@email.com
To: isaac-the-great@email.com
Subject: I saw you!

I saw you in the hallway. You were going into the elevator. Why didn't you wait? I called your name. Did you not hear me?

I was sad to see you leave. Did you get in trouble with the caseworker? Are you staying with Susan and John?

I have news. They're moving me. I admit

I'm scared. Now I'm the one scared all the time. Ms. Cutter said she "can't raise no delinquents."

I'm worried I will go somewhere bad, real bad. I'm scared I won't see Lucky anymore. I did what you said. I tried anyway. I asked Ms. Cutter if I could bake cookies. She said no. I told her I'd make some for her too. She still said no. She said to stay out of her kitchen.

It was a good idea, though. Thank you for the cookie recipe. I wish I could have tried. The cookies looked like they'd taste good. Maybe I can bake next week. If the new foster keepers let me.

I don't know anything about my new foster keepers. Maybe they will live closer to you. Then I would be farther from Lucky. But close to you. If we're better, maybe they will let us see each other. Hope so. Maybe my foster keepers will be like Susan and John?

I leave this weekend. Just four more days.

Fingers crossed

I am thinking of the good. Like I told you to do. Lucky gave me his email. I can write to him when I write to you.

He said he'll ask his mom if he can visit me if I move farther away.

I'll write more later. I want to hang out with Lucky as much as I can before I leave.

TTYS
Victor

2 Attachments
Lucky.jpg
My-sad-luggage.jpg

CHAPTER THIRTEEN
Following the Moon

From: isaac-the-great@email.com
To: victory333@email.com
Subject: Scrapbooks!!!!!

I didn't see or hear you. :(:'(

I'm sorry you're moving. But I'm glad you might be moving closer.

Is Mr. Burns okay? I'm happy I get to stay with Susan and John. I asked them if I could visit you. They said they are "open" for a visit. I think that means yes. Susan said she'd arrange it with the caseworker.

I'm sorry about Lucky, too. I like that picture of you two. Send me more. Susan said I can keep a photo album—a printed one! She said I can make scrapbooks. She makes scrapbooks all the time. Susan said she'll teach me. Momma would love that.

Remember how Momma kept saying she wanted to make fancy photo books? Susan said I can make more than one. I told her just two. One of our family—me, you, Vanessa, Sara, and Momma. The other one will be just for us brothers and our friends too. That photo of you and Lucky will be the first to go in.

Too bad you didn't get to try the cookies! Maybe I can send you some? Susan said I can mail food. I didn't know you could do that.

Susan and John teach me lots of things. Did I tell you John likes to take pictures? He takes pictures of everything. He is a photographer.

full moon

He took pictures of the full moon. I'll add it to the scrapbook. I'll put the moon right next to you and Lucky! :D

I know you worry about me forgetting Momma. I won't! No matter what Eric says. No matter how much I like Susan and John, they are not Momma. And I won't forget you, or our sisters. I promise.

I gotta go. Susan is calling me down to eat dinner. She made spaghetti. Susan puts sausage in her spaghetti!

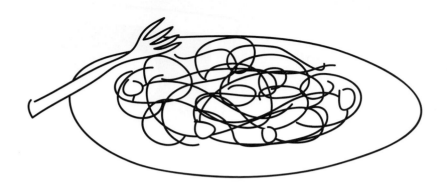

Weird, huh? But it actually tastes good.

~ Isaac

P.S. I hate that we were taken away. But maybe things will be okay.

P.P.S. Keep thinking of the good.

P.P.P.S. If we need to believe in something, we can believe in each other.

1 Attachment

moon.jpg

Want to Keep Reading?

Turn the page for a sneak peek at
the next book in the series.

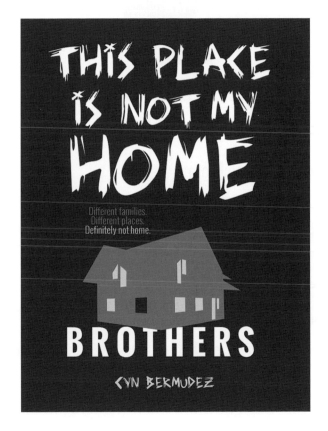

THIS PLACE
IS NOT MY
HOME

Different families.
Different places.
Definitely not home.

BROTHERS

CYN BERMUDEZ

ISBN: 9781538382318

CHAPTER ONE
How Far Is the Moon?

From: victory333@email.com
To: isaac-the-great@email.com
Subject: the new foster keepers

    I listened to records today. Do you remember what they are? Momma would play them when she cleaned house. Dad when he fixed cars. Momma used to have a bunch. Said they were "retro." She got rid of them when Dad died. You were five, halfway to six. I was seven. Records are how music was played in the olden days.

My new foster keepers collect records. They
have shelves full of them. I listened to Momma's
favorite song: "Moon River." Ugh…I used to hate
that song. But I really wanted to hear it today. You
know how rice reminds you of Momma? That
song reminds me of Momma. It made my chest
hurt, but I'd listen to it again if I could.

Listening to music was nice, even though I
missed Momma. We don't get to do much around
here. There are a lot of us. So it can get crazy
here.

My new foster keepers are real strict. They call it "controlled chaos." They have rules for everything! They have rules for the house. For us kids. For the things we share. Even for the few things that are our own.

Brian and Amy are my keepers. They live a few blocks from my first keeper, Ms. Cutter. At least I'm still at the same school with Lucky.

There are six of us kids. Mason, Rockford, and I are in one room. The girls, Cora, Boots, and Megs, are in another. Cora is the oldest. She's 16. Mason is the youngest, just five.

You should see this house! It's big and old and smelly. There are always noises. Usually one of the kids is making noise. Or Feather is singing (she's a bird). Or Boom is barking (he's a dog). But when it's supposed to be quiet, it's not. The floorboards creak whenever it's silent. It creaks the most at night when everyone is asleep. The paint outside and inside the house is peeling. I can hear the train rumbling by every night. It whistles so loud I think the house might fall apart one day.

But that's nothing compared to the way the wind whines. The way it rustles the old tree branches outside the bedroom window. The way it howls during a full moon. The way it sounds, some nights, like a woman crying. Mason thinks he sees shadows. He's always hiding under the covers at bedtime. Brian says the house is just settling. I don't believe him.

Sometimes, I'm glad for all the rules and chores. I don't have time to get too scared! Or let my imagination run away like last time…

All of us kids are cooking or cleaning, or we're at school. Lights out is the same for all of us. I'm usually so tired by the end of the day. We get an hour of free time. I'm glad they have a laptop. It takes forever to turn on, but it works. I'm going to email Lucky, too. Sometimes I sit out in the yard with Boom. He's my favorite. Brian and Amy have a bunch of pets:

- Boom Box – He's a gray boxer.
- Socks – He's an orange cat.
- Schrodinger – She's a black cat.
- Feather Fawcett – She's a yellow and white bird.
- Pork Chop – He's the goldfish. Actually, we don't know if he's a boy or a girl. I think he's a boy.

That's why Brian and Amy are "frugal," because there are a lot of mouths to feed. That's what Amy said. Momma would have called them cheap. They buy everything "no name." Like soap is just called soap. Not named soap, like how Momma would buy Zest. Anyway, it's okay I guess. Brian said it's just as good as anything named.

ABOUT THE AUTHOR

Cyn Bermudez is a writer from
Bakersfield, California. She attended
college in Santa Barbara, California,
where she studied physics, film,
and creative writing. Her work can
be found in anthologies such as
Building Red: Mission Mars, *The Best
of Vine Leaves Literary Journal* (2014),
and more. Her fiction and poetry
can also be found in *Middle Planet*,
Perihelion SF, *Strangelet*, *Mirror Dance*,
805 Literary and Art Journal, among
others. For more information about
Cyn, visit her website at
www.cynbermudez.com.

BROTHERS

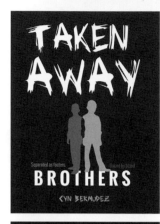

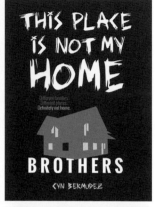

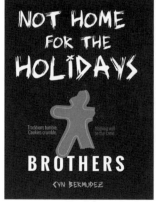

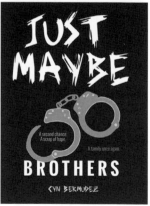

Check out more books at:

www.west44books.com

An imprint of Enslow Publishing

WEST 44 BOOKS™